Care Bears

Winter Wonderland

W9-BNA-499

By Justin Spelvin
Illustrated by Jay Johnson

Designed by Rick DeMonico

ISBN 0-439-66959-6

12 11 10 9 8 7 6 5 4 3   5 6 7 8 9/0
Printed in the U.S.A.
First printing, January 2005

SCHOLASTIC INC.
New York   Toronto   London   Auckland   Sydney
Mexico City   New Delhi   Hong Kong   Buenos Aires

A snowflake landed
on Tenderheart Bear.

"The first snow!"
he cheered. "It's time for
the Winter Festival!"

There was so much to do.
Tenderheart Bear made a list.

He gave each bear a job.

"What can I do?"
Cheer Bear asked.

"Come with me,"
Tenderheart Bear said.
"I'll find you a job."

Share Bear's job was snacks.
"I wanted to make snow cakes,"
said Share Bear.
"But I only have chocolate icing!"

"I know," said Cheer Bear.
"Sprinkle sugar on top."

"Great idea!" said Share Bear.

Wish Bear's job was music.
"I can't find my radio,"
said Wish Bear.

"What will we do?" asked
Tenderheart Bear.

"We could all sing,"
said Cheer Bear.

"Yes," said Wish Bear.
"And I have just the right song."

Champ Care Bear's job
was cleaning the ice.

"We can't go ice-skating,"
Champ said sadly.
"The pond's not frozen yet."

"I know," Cheer Bear said.
"We can roller-skate instead."

"What a good idea!"
said Champ Bear.

Grumpy Bear's job
was building snowbears.

"Oh, dear," said Grumpy Bear.
"This is too heavy for me."

"We can all try,"
Cheer Bear said.
"One, two, three . . ."

The head fit just right.
"Thanks," said Grumpy Bear.

The big festival banner
hung from the trees.

CARE-A-LOT

FEST

"What else should I put up?"
Bedtime Bear asked.

"Stars are cheery,"
said Cheer Bear.
It was a great idea.

So they hung stars
from every tree.

"I never got a job,"
said Cheer Bear.

"No, not one job,"
Tenderheart Bear said.
"Instead, you helped us all!"

Cheer Bear smiled.

Soon Care-a-lot was filled
with singing, roller-skating,
snowbears, and tasty treats.

CARE-A-LOT WINTER
FESTIVAL

It was the best
Winter Festival ever.

CARE-A-LOT WINTER
FESTIVAL